This book belongs to:

...........................................................

Brimax Publishing
415 Jackson St, San Francisco
CA 94111 USA
www.brimax.com.au

# The
# Ugly Duckling

*Illustrated by*
## Sue Lisansky

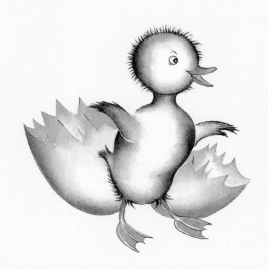

**M**other Duck had five eggs in her nest. She was waiting for them to hatch. Soon, four of the eggs hatched and out came four fluffy yellow ducklings. But the last egg did not hatch.

"It's a goose egg," said the chicken.

"It's not a goose egg," said the goose. "It's a turkey egg."

"How will I know?" asked Mother Duck.

"It won't swim," said the goose. "Turkeys cannot swim."

The egg hatched and a funny little duckling came out. He was gray and fuzzy.

He went straight to the pond and swam with his brothers and sisters.

The other birds in the farmyard laughed at the ugly duckling. He was so unhappy that he ran away.

He went to a big lake, but the wild ducks chased him away. He lived alone all summer.

One day he saw some beautiful white swans flying above the lake.

"I wish I were a swan," he said. "No one laughs at swans."

When winter came the ducks flew away. The ugly
duckling stayed by the lake. It was very cold and
snow began to fall.

He was very sad and lonely.

One night it was so cold that the ugly duckling was trapped in the ice.

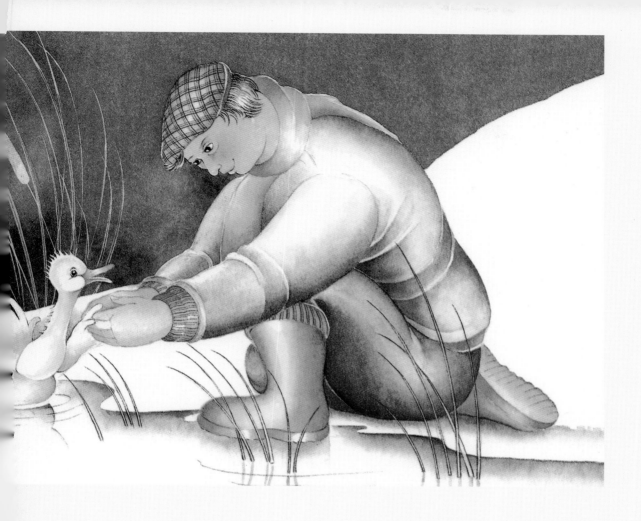

The next morning, a farmer out walking with his dog broke the ice and freed him.

When spring came, the wild ducks returned to the lake.

They splashed and played in the water.

The ugly duckling wanted to make friends but he was too scared to go up to the wild ducks.

"I wish they would talk to me," he said. "I will look for a new home far away." He flew up into the sky for the first time.

He flapped his large wings and flew over the land.
Below him he saw some swans swimming on a pond.
He flew down to them.

He swam up to the group of swans.

"I am ugly and lonely," he said. "Will you be my friends?"

"You are not ugly," said the swans. "Look at
yourself in the pond. You are a swan, like us.
Of course we will be your friends!"

The ugly duckling looked and saw that he was a swan.

He was so happy! Then two children came to the pond.

"Look at the new swan!" they said. "He is beautiful!"

The new swan knew he would never be lonely again.

# NOTE TO PARENTS

The *First Fairy Tales* series is specially designed to help improve your child's literacy and reading comprehension. The following activities will help you discuss the story with your child, and will make the experience of reading more pleasurable.

## Here are some key words in the story. Can you read them?

egg        farmer

nest       dog

duck      snow

duckling   ice

goose     children

swan

pond

## How much of the story can you remember?

Did the ugly duckling look like his brothers and sisters?

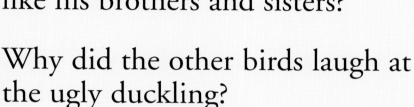

Why did the other birds laugh at the ugly duckling?

Where did the ugly duckling go when he ran away?

What did the ugly duckling want to be?

Who helped the ugly duckling when he got trapped in the ice?

What did the swans say to the ugly duckling?

Who came to the pond to visit the swans?